Pollyanna

*Retold from the Eleanor H. Porter original
by Kathleen Olmstead*

Illustrated by Jamel Akib

Sterling Publishing Co., Inc.
New York

Library of Congress Cataloging-in-Publication Data

Olmstead, Kathleen.
 Pollyanna / retold from the Eleanor H. Porter original by Kathleen Olmstead ;
illustrated by Jamel Akib ; afterword by Arthur Pober.
      p. cm.—(Classic starts)
 Summary: An abridged version of the tale of orphaned, eleven-year-old
Pollyanna, who comes to live with austere and wealthy Aunt Polly, bringing
happiness to her aunt and other members of the community through her
philosophy of gladness.
 ISBN-13: 978-1-4027-3692-6
 ISBN-10: 1-4027-3692-4
 [1. Orphans—Fiction. 2. Aunts—Fiction. 3. Conduct of life—Fiction. 4.
Cheerfulness—Fiction. 5. Interpersonal relations—Fiction. 6. Vermont—
History—20th century—Fiction.] I. Akib, Jamel, ill. II. Pober, Arthur. III.
Porter, Eleanor H. (Eleanor Hodgman), 1868–1920. Pollyanna. IV. Title. V. Series.

PZ7.O499Pol 2007
[Fic]—dc22

                                                              2006014768

                          2 4 6 8 10 9 7 5 3 1

                        Published by Sterling Publishing Co., Inc.
                        387 Park Avenue South, New York, NY 10016
                          Copyright © 2007 by Kathleen Olmstead
                         Illustrations copyright © 2007 by Jamel Akib
                          Distributed in Canada by Sterling Publishing
                        ᶜ/ₒ Canadian Manda Group, 165 Dufferin Street,
                               Toronto, Ontario, Canada M6K 3H6
                Distributed in the United Kingdom by GMC Distribution Services,
                Castle Place, 166 High Street, Lewes, East Sussex, England BN7 1XU
                    Distributed in Australia by Capricorn Link (Australia) Pty. Ltd.
                             P.O. Box 704, Windsor, NSW 2756, Australia

                    Classic Starts is a trademark of Sterling Publishing Co., Inc.

                        Sterling ISBN-13: 978-1-4027-3692-6
                              ISBN-10: 1-4027-3692-4

                For information about custom editions, special sales, premium and
                      corporate purchases, please contact Sterling Special Sales
                Department at 800-805-5489 or specialsales@sterlingpub.com.

CONTENTS

❧

CHAPTER 1

Miss Polly

⌒

One June morning, Miss Polly Harrington rushed into her kitchen. This was not her usual manner. Miss Polly did not like to rush. Normally, she was a very careful and well-mannered woman.

Nancy was standing at the sink washing dishes. She watched Miss Polly dart around the room. In the two months that Nancy had been working at the house, she had never seen Miss Polly so active.

"Nancy!" Miss Polly called.

"Yes, ma'am," Nancy answered. She turned to look at Miss Polly but did not stop washing the dishes.

"Nancy," Miss Polly said. Her voice was very stern. "I wish you would stop working when I'm talking to you. I need your full attention."

Nancy blushed. She put the dish down on the counter. She almost knocked it over as she turned around but caught it just in time. Miss Polly always made her nervous. Nancy was so worried about making a mistake.

"I'm sorry, ma'am," she said. "I kept working because you said I should work quickly today. It was important to get everything done."

Miss Polly frowned. "I did not ask you for an explanation," she said. "I asked you to pay attention."

Nancy tried not to sigh. This was her first job. Her mother was a widow, and Nancy had three younger siblings. The family needed money, so

Nancy found a job at the big house on the hill. She knew that Miss Polly was one of the richest people in the county. She also knew that Miss Polly ran the Harrington estate. Now, after two months of working for Miss Polly Harrington, Nancy also knew that she was a very strict and tough boss.

Miss Polly was always quick to complain if a door slammed or a fork fell to the floor. She always commented on dusty tables and wrinkled uniforms. But she never took the time to tell you if something was done well. She did not smile. She did not compliment. But Nancy swallowed her pride and worked hard for Miss Polly every day.

"When you are finished with the dishes," Miss Polly continued, "I want you to clear out the back attic room. Remove the trunks and boxes and set up a cot." Miss Polly paused for a moment. "You will need to sweep the floor, of course."

"Of course," Nancy said.

"I might as well tell you," Miss Polly said, "my niece, Pollyanna Whittier, is coming to live with me. She is eleven years old and will sleep in the back attic room."

"A young girl?" Nancy said. "How nice!" Nancy was thinking about her own little sisters. They brought such joy to her life and she missed them very much.

"Nice?" Miss Polly sniffed. "That's not how I would describe it. However, I intend to make the best of it. I am a good woman, and I know my duty."

Nancy blushed once again. "Of course," she said quietly. "I only meant that a little girl might brighten things up a bit. She might be good company for you."

"Thank you," Miss Polly said coldly. "I don't think I have an immediate need for company."

"But you must want to see her?" Nancy said. "She is your sister's child, after all." Nancy realized she might have to welcome this lonely little girl on her own.

Miss Polly held her head high and looked sternly at her servant. "If my sister was silly enough to marry and bring yet another child into this world—when we have more than enough already—that is her business. I can't see why I must now be responsible for it—I mean her. However, as I've said, I know my duty."

Miss Polly turned to leave. She paused at the doorway and looked back at Nancy. "Make sure you clean all the corners in the living room," she said. "I don't want to see any dust on the furniture."

"Yes, ma'am," Nancy said. Then she turned back to the sink to finish the dishes.

Miss Polly sat at the desk in her room. She took a letter out of the drawer and read it. She had read this letter many times over the past two days. She had been very surprised by its arrival.

It was addressed to Miss Polly Harrington, Beldingsville, Vermont, and read as follows:

Dear Madam,

I regret to inform you that your brother-in-law, the Reverend John Whittier, died two weeks ago. He left one child, an eleven-year-old daughter. He owned very little, other than a few books. As you know, he was the pastor for this small parish and had a very small salary.

I understand that he was your deceased sister's husband. He told me that your families were not on the best of terms. However, he thought you might wish to take the child for your sister's sake. Therefore, I am writing to you.

Please let me know if you can take the child. There is a couple from the parish heading east soon. They could bring Pollyanna as far as Boston. We will tell you which train from Boston to Beldingsville she will arrive on.

Hoping to hear a favorable response from you soon,

Respectfully yours,
Jeremiah O. White

Miss Polly folded the letter and slipped it back inside the envelope. She had already sent word that she would take the child. What else could she do? It was an unpleasant task, but she could not ignore her responsibilities.

She thought about her sister Jennie, the child's mother. Jennie had only been twenty years old when she insisted on marrying the young reverend. The whole family objected to the match, but Jennie was stubborn. She had other suitors—including a very wealthy man that the family approved of—but Jennie was not interested. The reverend had no money, but he did have a great deal of youthful enthusiasm and

7

a heart full of love. Jennie married the reverend and went west with him as a missionary's wife.

Miss Polly had only been fifteen when her sister left, but she still remembered it well. Jennie had written often for the first few years. She told the family about her husband and children. Unfortunately, all of her children died except the last little girl, Pollyanna. Jennie had named her daughter after her two sisters, Polly and Anna. But Mr. and Mrs. Harrington had refused to respond to Jennie's letters and eventually the letters stopped coming. A few years later, the family received a sad note from the reverend saying Jennie had died.

It had been twenty-five years since Jennie had left home. Miss Polly was now forty years old. Even though she still lived in the big house on the hill, many things had changed. She was now all alone in the world. Her father, mother, and sisters had all died. Some people suggested she find a friend or companion to live with her in the big house. They all thought she was lonely. But she always refused. She insisted that she was not lonely. She preferred quiet.

Miss Polly stood up from her desk and frowned. She was glad, of course, to be of some service and to do her duty, but Pollyanna! What a ridiculous name!

∾

Nancy worked very hard in the little attic room. She scrubbed and cleaned everywhere, being extra careful in the corners. In truth, Nancy was working out her stress and frustration. "How dare she stick that precious little child in this hot room," she muttered. "And there's no fire for the winter, either. This is such a big house with so many rooms."

When Nancy was finished, she looked around the room in disgust. "Well, I've done my part, then. There's no more dirt in this room." Nancy sighed. "As a matter of fact, there's not much of anything. The poor little girl will be so homesick and lonely when she arrives. This room will not be a happy welcome."

Nancy left the room, slamming the door behind her. She jumped at the sound, realizing that Miss Polly might get upset. She shook her head quickly. "Never mind, then. I hope she did hear the bang!" she said out loud. She paused and wondered if Miss Polly had heard her speak. Nancy shook her head again and headed back to work.

That afternoon, Nancy walked into the garden to talk to Old Tom. He had worked as Miss Polly's gardener for many years.

"Tom," Nancy said. She looked over her shoulder to make sure no one else was nearby to hear. "Did you know that a little girl is coming to live here?"

"A—what?" Tom demanded. He stood up straight. It was difficult for the old man. He spent so much of his day bent over grass and weeds.

"A little girl," Nancy replied.

"Don't be ridiculous." Tom shook his head. "Whatever would Miss Polly do with a little girl? I've never heard of anything so silly."

"But it's true," Nancy insisted. "She told me so herself. I just fixed up the attic room. It's Miss Polly's niece and she's eleven years old."

The man's jaw fell. There was a tender look in his eyes. Tom looked at Nancy and smiled. "It has to be Miss Jennie's girl! She was the only one to get married. I can't believe it! Miss Jennie's girl is coming here."

Nancy was confused. "Who's Miss Jennie?" she asked.

"She was an angel straight out of heaven," he said. "Miss Jennie was the oldest daughter of

Mr. and Mrs. Harrington. She got married real young and left home. How old did you say her little girl was?"

"Eleven years old," Nancy said.

Tom smiled slowly. "I do wonder what Miss Polly will do with a child in the house. It will be a very different place."

"Humph! Well, I'm wondering what a child will do with Miss Polly in the house!" snapped Nancy.

The old man laughed. "You aren't so fond of Miss Polly, are you?" he said, chuckling.

"As if anybody could be fond of her," she replied with a sniff.

Tom smiled again as he bent back down over his work. "I guess you haven't heard anything about Miss Polly's long-lost love."

"A long-lost love? Miss Polly? No, I haven't heard anything about that." Nancy was shocked by Tom's comment. "I can't imagine anybody else has heard about that either."

"Oh, yes, they have," Tom nodded. "And the fellow still lives here, too."

"Who is he?" Nancy asked. She hated to miss a good story.

"Oh, I'm not going to tell," Tom said. "It's none of my business." Tom stood straight again. He looked at the big house. He had worked for the Harringtons for many years. Tom was proud of his service and felt loyal to his employers.

"But it doesn't seem possible." Nancy said and shook her head. "I can't imagine her loving anybody. Or anybody loving her."

"You don't know Miss Polly as I do," Tom said. "She was once a very pretty young woman. She used to wear fancy dresses and put flowers in her hair. She still could be pretty if she wanted. Miss Polly's not old, you know."

"Isn't she?" Nancy asked. "She sure acts like an old lady."

"I know," Tom said. "She started to act that way right after she began fighting with her suitor."

"There's just no pleasing her," Nancy said. It was hard working for Miss Polly. "If it weren't for the fact that my mother and sisters depend on my salary to get by, I would never stay. Someday, you know, I'm going to lose my temper."

"I know," Tom said. "It's hard for everyone. Just be careful, though. You don't want to rock the boat."

Nancy was about to answer when she heard her name.

"Nancy!" called a sharp voice.

"Yes, ma'am," Nancy answered. She turned and ran toward the house.

CHAPTER 2

The Coming of Pollyanna

ᴄᴏ

Miss Polly climbed the stairs. She walked into the attic room and sighed. Pollyanna would arrive soon.

She looked around the room. There was a small bed, a chair, a washstand, a dresser, and a small table. There were no pictures on the walls. There was nothing that looked warm or welcoming.

The room was also very hot. There were no drapes on the windows, so sunshine poured right in. There were no screens on the windows, so they remained closed. A fly was buzzing against a closed window trying to get out. Miss Polly quickly killed it. She opened the window a tiny bit to throw it outside. She frowned once more, then left the room.

Miss Polly found Nancy in the kitchen. "I found a fly in Miss Pollyanna's room," she said. "That means the windows must have been open at some point. I have ordered new screens, but until then I want the windows to remain closed."

Nancy quietly said, "Yes, ma'am."

"I will need you to go with Timothy to the station this afternoon," Miss Polly said. "You can take the horse and buggy. The telegram said she has light hair, a red gingham dress, and a straw hat. I'm afraid that is all I know."

"Of course, ma'am. But shouldn't you be the one . . ."

"No," Miss Polly said. She sounded angry. "I will not be going to the train station. It is not necessary."

At precisely twenty minutes to four that afternoon, Nancy and Timothy left for the station. Timothy was Tom's son. It was often said that if Tom was Miss Polly's right-hand man, then Timothy was her left.

Timothy was a very nice young man. Many people said that he was handsome, too. Although Nancy had only worked at the house for a short time, she and Timothy were already good friends. Today, however, Nancy was not in a talkative mood. She sat quietly in the buggy all the way to the station. When they arrived, she jumped out and headed for the platform.

Timothy walked up beside Nancy. "I wonder what she's going to be like," he said. "Can you imagine what will happen if she is a noisy kid? Miss Polly wouldn't take it very well."

They heard the train's whistle as it pulled into the station.

"Timothy," Nancy said sadly, "she shouldn't

have sent me. It's not right. Miss Polly should be here to meet her niece."

Soon Nancy saw a young girl—light hair, gingham dress, and straw hat—step off the train. Her face was freckled and eager. The girl looked up and down the platform as if searching for someone.

It took Nancy a few minutes to raise her courage to say hello. She walked up to the girl and stuttered, "M-m-miss P-P-Pollyanna?" Before Nancy had a chance to say another word, she was wrapped in the little girl's arms.

"Oh, I'm so pleased that you came to meet me!" Pollyanna gushed. "I hoped that you would come and here you are. I couldn't be happier. I'm so glad, glad, GLAD!"

"Y-you are?" Nancy said. She looked over at Timothy, confused.

"I thought about you the whole trip. I wondered what you would look like." Pollyanna

began to dance around Nancy. She stood on her toes and swung her arms about her. "And now I know and I'm glad you look just as you look."

Poor Nancy was very confused by all of Pollyanna's words and dancing. She was not certain what she should do next.

Thankfully, Timothy walked up beside her.

"This is Timothy," Nancy said. "Maybe you have a trunk?"

"Yes, I do," Pollyanna said proudly. "The Ladies' Aid bought it for me. And wasn't it lovely of them when they really needed to buy a new carpet? I have no idea how much a new carpet might cost, but I'm sure it isn't very cheap. Oh, and I have this piece of paper in my bag. Mr. Gray said it was a check and that I must give it to you right away. Mr. Gray is Mrs. Gray's husband. I came east with them, and they are lovely!" Pollyanna reached into her bag and pulled out the check. She handed it to Nancy.

Nancy drew a long breath. She felt that some-one had to breathe deeply after that long speech. She looked quickly at Timothy, but he turned away. Neither one wanted to break the news that Miss Polly had not come to meet the girl.

Timothy found her trunk, and they left the train station. Pollyanna sat between them on the buggy seat. She asked a stream of questions. In fact, she did not stop talking the entire way home.

"I hope it isn't too far," Pollyanna said. "I won't mind so much if it is, of course, but I would like to be home. It will be a lovely ride, though. My goodness, what a pretty street," Pollyanna exclaimed. "I knew that it would be. Father told me Beldingsville was a beautiful town."

Pollyanna stopped talking for a moment. Nancy turned to see what was wrong. She saw that the little girl had tears in her eyes and her chin was shaking. Pollyanna only paused a moment, though. Soon she was back to her constant chatter.

"Father told me all about it. He remembered everything about Beldingsville. Oh, wait," Pollyanna said. "I forgot to explain about this gingham dress. Mrs. Gray said that I should tell you right away. You might think it's strange that I'm wearing gingham rather than black. There just wasn't any black material in the church's supply to make me a mourning dress. Someone suggested buying me a black dress and hat, but it might have been expensive. Besides, Mrs. Gray said that she didn't like children in black. I mean, she liked children, of course, but not children wearing black."

"Well, I'm sure it will be all right," Nancy said. She was surprised that she managed to get a word in.

"I'm glad that you feel that way," Pollyanna

said. "I do, too. Of course, it would be a good deal harder to be glad in black."

"Glad?" Nancy gasped.

"Yes. Father has gone to heaven to be with Mother and the rest, you know. He said I must be glad. It's been pretty hard to do it—even in the red gingham. I miss him terribly and wish I could be with all of them, too. I was all alone after he died. I only had the Ladies' Aid. But now I'm sure it will be easier because I've got you, Aunt Polly. I'm so glad I've got you!"

"Oh no! You've made a mistake," Nancy said. She felt panicked. "I'm only Nancy. I'm not your Aunt Polly at all!"

"You—you aren't?" stammered the little girl. She was clearly saddened by the news.

"No, I'm only Nancy," she said. "I should have said so back at the station. Your Aunt Polly and I aren't a bit alike. Not one bit."

"But who *are* you then?" Pollyanna asked. "You don't look like someone from the Ladies' Aid."

Timothy burst out laughing.

"I'm the hired girl. I do all the work around the house, except for laundry. Miss Durgin takes care of the laundry." Nancy tried not to look bothered by Timothy's laughter.

"But there is an Aunt Polly, isn't there?" demanded the child.

"You bet your life there is," Timothy said. He continued to chuckle under his breath.

Pollyanna relaxed.

"Oh, that's all right, then." Pollyanna sat quietly for no more than fifteen seconds. "And you know, I'm glad that she didn't come meet me. I can still look forward to meeting her now. And I've also got you!" She looked at Nancy and smiled.

Nancy blushed. Timothy looked at her with a smile.

"I'd say that's a pretty nice compliment," he said. "Why don't you thank the little lady?"

"I—I—I was just thinking about Miss Polly," Nancy said slowly.

"I was, too," Pollyanna said, sighing. "I'm very interested and curious about her. You know, she's the only aunt I've got. I didn't know anything about her until a short while ago. Father said that she lived in a big house way on top of a hill."

"Look, you can see it now," Nancy said.

"Oh my, how pretty it is!" Pollyanna said. "There are so many trees! I never saw such green grass in all my life. Is Aunt Polly rich, Nancy?"

"Yes, miss."

"I'm so glad. I've never known anyone with a lot of money—except the White family. They had a lot of money. There were carpets in every room and ice cream on Sundays. Does Aunt Polly have ice cream on Sundays?"

Nancy shook her head. She avoided looking at Timothy, who was laughing again. "No. I guess Miss Polly doesn't like ice cream. At least I've never seen any in the house."

Pollyanna's face fell.

"That is so sad! How could anyone not like ice cream?" Pollyanna thought for a moment. "But what about the carpets? Does she have carpets in every room?"

"Yes, she has carpets," Nancy replied. "In almost every room," she added. Nancy was thinking about the bare room in the attic where Pollyanna would sleep. There were no carpets in that room.

"Oh, I'm so glad." Pollyanna clapped her hands. "I love carpets! We didn't have any. We only had two little rugs that the church gave us. Mrs. White also had a lot of pictures. Don't you just love pictures?"

"I don't really know," Nancy said. So many of Pollyanna's questions confused her.

"I love pictures. We didn't have any, of course. There aren't so many pictures at a church that they can donate them. They only gave us pictures twice. One time the picture was so nice that Father sold it to buy some shoes. The other one was so bad that it fell to pieces as soon as we hung it up. The glass, I mean. It was the glass that broke. I cried so much when the picture broke. We had so few pretty things."

The buggy pulled into the driveway at Miss Polly's. Pollyanna pointed at the house again. "Oh, it is such a beautiful house, isn't it?"

As Timothy unloaded the trunk, Nancy whispered in his ear. "I'll never say another word about leaving this job again. My work just became very interesting."

"I'll say," Timothy added. "With that little girl around, this house will be more fun than the fair!"

CHAPTER 3

The Little Attic Room

co

Miss Polly looked up from her book as Nancy and Pollyanna walked into the living room. She did not get up. Instead, she held her hand out toward her niece as a polite greeting. "How do you do, Pollyanna? I am your——"

Miss Polly did not have a chance to finish her sentence. Pollyanna flew across the room. She threw her arms around her aunt and hugged her tightly.

"Oh, Aunt Polly," the young girl sobbed. "It is so wonderful to be here. I am so glad. You have no idea how happy I am to be here with you and Nancy. It was so hard just having the Ladies' Aid."

"I don't suppose I would have any idea," Miss Polly sniffed. She tried to pull the little girl's arms away.

"Nancy, you may go now," Miss Polly said. "Pollyanna! Please stand up straight."

Pollyanna stepped back immediately. She giggled. "Oh, Aunt Polly, I have so many things to tell you. I should probably start with my gingham dress and why I'm not wearing black. I already told Nancy that my father told me . . ."

"Never mind what your father said," Miss Polly interrupted. She spoke sharply. "I suppose you brought a trunk with you."

"Oh yes," Pollyanna said. "The Ladies' Aid was kind enough to buy it for me. I didn't have many clothes to bring. We never had much money, you see. We had to get my clothes from the charity box. Unfortunately, there aren't many clothes for girls my age. But I brought all of my father's books. Mrs. White thought I should keep them, so we packed them in the trunk."

"Pollyanna," her aunt interrupted her once again. "We should be clear about one thing. I do not care for you mentioning your father to me."

Pollyanna gasped. "But Aunt Polly, what do you mean?"

"There's nothing more to discuss. I'll take you up to your room now." Miss Polly stood up. "Please follow me upstairs."

Poor Pollyanna followed her aunt out of the room. Her eyes were brimming with tears, but she bravely held her chin high.

Pollyanna tried to convince herself that it would be all right. *Maybe it will be better if I don't speak about Father*, she thought to herself. *It might be easier if I don't think about him. That must be why Aunt Polly doesn't want me to talk about him. She knows it will just make me sad.* Now that Pollyanna was sure her aunt was acting out of kindness, she wiped away her tears.

The little girl looked at the pictures on the walls and the carpet on the floor. "Aunt Polly, I can hardly believe how beautiful everything is! You must be glad that you're so rich!"

"Pollyanna!" Miss Polly stopped in her tracks. "How dare you speak to me like that!"

"Why?" Pollyanna asked. "Aren't you terribly rich?"

"I most certainly am not!" Miss Polly said. "I do hope that I would never be sinfully proud of any of God's gifts, certainly not riches."

Miss Polly continued to walk down the hall. She was glad that she had decided to put the girl in the attic room. At first, she just wanted to keep her far away. Miss Polly also worried that the girl would destroy the good furniture. Now she was glad to give her the plain room. It might teach Pollyanna a lesson or two about pride.

Pollyanna quickly forgot how sharply her aunt had spoken to her. She was already entertaining herself. She wondered which of the beautiful doors would lead to her new room. Everything looked so wonderful. She could not wait to see her bed and the pictures on the walls.

Miss Polly finally opened one of the doors. It led to another staircase. Pollyanna followed her aunt up the stairs. There was another small hallway at the top. Miss Polly stepped into the room on the right.

The room was positively bare. There was nothing on the walls and only a few pieces of furniture. Pollyanna was so disappointed and confused that she could barely speak.

"I think you have everything you need," Miss Polly said. "Timothy has already brought up your trunk. Do you have the key?"

Pollyanna stared at her aunt for a moment. She slowly nodded her head.

"Pollyanna," her aunt said, "When I ask a question, I expect an answer. Nodding your head is not enough."

"Yes, Aunt Polly," she said.

"Very well, then," Miss Polly said. "I'll send Nancy up to help you unpack. Dinner is at six."

Miss Polly left the room without another word.

Pollyanna stared at her bare walls for a few moments. There was nothing to look at. Then she looked at her trunk. It reminded her of home. She walked quickly to the trunk and fell down beside it. She held her head in her hands and cried.

Nancy walked in to see the little girl weeping over her trunk. "Oh, Pollyanna," she said. "I was worried that I would find you like this."

Nancy crouched beside the girl and stroked her hair. "There, there, you poor lamb."

Pollyanna shook her head. "I'm an awful and wicked girl, Nancy," she cried. "I just can't understand why God and the angels need my father more than I do."

"Now, now," Nancy said gently. "Where's the key to your trunk. We can start unpacking. You'll feel a bit better when you're settled in."

Pollyanna took a key from her pocket and handed it to Nancy. "I'm afraid that there isn't much to unpack, though. I don't own many dresses."

"Well then, we'll be finished that much sooner," Nancy said.

Pollyanna smiled brightly. "Yes! That's true isn't it?" She gave Nancy a quick hug. "I can be glad about that, can't I?"

Once again, Nancy was confused by Pollyanna's excitement. Only a moment ago she had been crying and now she was bright and happy. Nancy was quite certain that she had never met anyone like Pollyanna before.

Nancy and Pollyanna got to work. Nancy pulled things from the trunk, and Pollyanna put them away. Her very plain, slightly worn dresses were hung in the closet. The books were lined up on the dresser. The undergarments went in the drawers.

"I think it is a very nice room, don't you?" Pollyanna said bravely.

Nancy did not reply.

"And I'm glad that there isn't a mirror because then I would have to look at my freckles."

"You always find a reason to be glad," Nancy said. "Nothing seems to bother you for long."

Pollyanna giggled softly. "Well, it's a game that I play."

"A game?" Nancy asked.

"I call it the Just Be Glad game," Pollyanna said. "Father taught it to me. I've been playing it for years. I taught it to the women in the Ladies' Aid, and they played it, too. Well, some of them played."

"Okay, then," Nancy said. "How do you play this game?"

"It's very simple, really," Pollyanna said. "You must find something in everything to be glad about."

Nancy shook her head to say that she did not understand.

"For instance," Pollyanna continued. "If you see a pair of crutches, just be glad that you don't need them. That's all there is to it. Of course, sometimes it's very hard to find something to make you glad. Father going to live with the angels and leaving me with no one but the Ladies' Aid was hard. But that meant I came here to meet Aunt Polly and you."

"And now you're stuck in an attic room with no pictures," Nancy snapped.

"Yes," Pollyanna said slowly. "That was hard at first. I was feeling very lonely. But then I thought how I hate to look at my freckles in a mirror. I knew that I would find more things to be glad about. Once you start looking for the happy things, you don't think about the bad ones as much."

Nancy did not respond. She had to swallow hard to stop herself from crying.

"Of course, it's a lot easier when you have someone to play with," Pollyanna said. "Father and I used to play all the time. Maybe Aunt Polly would play with me."

"My stars and stockings!" Nancy said. "Miss Polly? No, I don't think she's one for games." Nancy sniffed loudly. She could not picture

Miss Polly Harrington playing the Just Be Glad game.

Nancy continued to work in silence, while Pollyanna walked to the window. The girl started to clap her hands and giggle with joy. "Oh, I didn't notice this before!" she said. "Look at this view. There's a church spire and a river shining like silver. I don't need pictures hanging on my wall when I can look out my window. Oh, Nancy, I'm so glad she gave me this room now!"

All of a sudden, Nancy burst into tears.

"Nancy, whatever could be wrong?" Pollyanna ran to her side to comfort her. She hugged her new friend. "Oh no, this wasn't your room, was it?"

"My room?" Nancy scoffed. "Of course not!"

They both turned at the sound of a bell. "That's your aunt calling," Nancy said. She sprang to her feet and rushed downstairs.

Pollyanna turned back to her "picture."

While staring out the window, she suddenly noticed how hot the room was. She pushed the window up. Pollyanna then leaned out the window. She took deep breaths of the fresh, sweet air.

Then she went to the other window and did the same thing. She opened it up wide and leaned out. Several flies flew into to the room, but Pollyanna did not mind. She was too busy staring at the tree just outside her window.

Later that night when she was tucked into her bed, Pollyanna felt scared and alone. This was her first night here. She missed her old house, her father, and even the Ladies' Aid. She looked out her window at the tree and did her best to play the Just Be Glad game. "If I didn't come to live with Aunt Polly," she whispered to herself. "I would never have seen this beautiful tree." Pollyanna fell asleep thinking about moonlight shining on its branches and leaves.

CHAPTER 4

A Question of Duty

౿

Pollyanna woke up just before seven the next
morning. She could see blue sky out her window.
A light cool breeze was coming into the room. She
knew it was going to be a beautiful day.

She walked to the window and looked over
the garden. Her aunt Polly was already outside
walking among the plants. Pollyanna dressed
quickly and ran downstairs to greet her.

Miss Polly was talking to Tom about the
rosebushes. Pollyanna ran up behind her and
threw her arms around her waist.

"Good morning, Aunt Polly!" the little girl said. "Isn't it a lovely day?"

Miss Polly stood up straight, pushing Pollyanna back. "Is this how you usually say good morning?"

Pollyanna giggled and danced around her aunt. "No, only when I love someone so much I just can't help it. I saw you from my window and remembered that you weren't someone from the Ladies' Aid but my honest to goodness aunt. I was just so excited that I ran all the way down here."

"Oh my goodness," Miss Polly said. She tried to frown, but it was not so easy. "That's all for now, Tom. Please do as I say with the roses."

Pollyanna looked at the old man. "Do you always work in the garden, Mr.—Mr.—man?" she asked.

He turned to look at her. There were tears in his eyes because she reminded him of Miss Jennie. "Yes, miss," he said. "My name is Tom.

I'm the gardener. I've worked here for many, many years."

He reached out a hand to touch Pollyanna's hair. "You look just like your mother," he said quietly. "I knew her when she was even younger than you."

Pollyanna's eyes grew wide. "You knew my mother?" she said, amazed. "Please tell me everything about her!"

The girl sat down in the dirt path beside Tom. She waited patiently for him to start talking. Just then a bell sounded.

Nancy rushed out the back door. "Miss Pollyanna," she called. "That's the breakfast bell." She grabbed the girl's hand and pulled her toward the house. "You can't be late, miss."

After breakfast, Miss Polly followed her niece to the attic room. "Please show me your dresses. Whatever is not appropriate will be given to the needy."

Pollyanna slowly moved to her closet. "I'm afraid there isn't much," she said softly. "All of my clothes came from donations. There weren't many dresses given to me lately. Have you ever had to rely on charity for your clothes, Aunt Polly?"

Miss Polly looked at her niece with shock.

Pollyanna quickly realized her mistake. "Oh, no, I don't suppose you have. Rich people never have to rely on charity. I'm sorry. I guess being up in this room, I forgot that you are rich."

Miss Polly continued to stare at Pollyanna. The girl kept talking.

"Well, I was just going to say that you never know what you'll find in a donation barrel. There weren't always a lot of dresses to choose from. It was hard to play the game then, but Father used to say . . ." Pollyanna remembered that she was not supposed to mention her father.

Miss Polly went to the closet and looked over each garment slowly. Pollyanna was right. They were not pretty dresses. It was hard to believe that any of them even fit the girl. Miss Polly examined the rest of her niece's things and came to the same conclusion. All of the girl's clothes were in a similar condition.

"Have you been to school?" Miss Polly asked.

"Yes, Aunt Polly," Pollyanna answered. "Also, Father taught me at home. I mean, yes, I have been to school."

"That's fine. We will put you in school in the fall. Hopefully you will be able to be in the proper grade. I suppose you should read to me for a half hour every day to prepare."

"I love to read, Aunt Polly," the girl said. "I would like that very much. And I don't mind reading on my own. I actually prefer it because of the big words. I like sounding them out all on my own."

"I'm sure you do," Miss Polly said. It was hard to keep up with the girl's strange stories. "What about cooking?"

"Well, we didn't get very far with that," Pollyanna said. "The Ladies' Aid couldn't decide if I should learn how to cook or to sew. They argued endlessly about it. Finally it was decided that I should take one cooking lesson and then one sewing lesson. But the only thing I learned how to make before I had to leave was chocolate-and-fig cake."

"Chocolate-and-fig cake?" Miss Polly said. "There's not much use for that."

Pollyanna shrugged her shoulders in response.

"All right. At nine o'clock every morning, you will read to me for thirty minutes. Two days a week you will spend your mornings with Nancy learning how to cook. You will spend the other mornings with me learning how to sew. You will spend the afternoons on music lessons.

I should probably arrange a tutor for you, as well. Who knows what kind of schooling you've had so far."

"But Aunt Polly," Pollyanna exclaimed, "you haven't left me any time for living."

"Living? My goodness, what are you talking about?" Miss Polly frowned. "As if you weren't living all the time."

"Of course, I'd be breathing while I was doing all those things, but I wouldn't be living." Pollyanna clasped her hands together. "I need time to talk with Nancy and Old Tom in the garden. To wander through the town and fields and find out about people and houses and everything. That is what I call living, Aunt Polly. Just breathing isn't living."

Miss Polly shook her head. "Pollyanna, you are the most extraordinary girl I've ever met. Of course, you will be allowed a proper amount of playtime. But if I am willing to do my duty to feed and clothe and care for you, I think you should meet me halfway."

Pollyanna looked shocked. "I'm sorry, Aunt Polly. I didn't mean to be ungrateful. I love you!"

"Very well," Miss Polly said. "Then be sure not to act ungrateful."

Miss Polly stood up. "Timothy will take us into town at one o'clock. We'll need to pick up material for new clothes. None of these dresses will do. I can't have my niece seen in such rags. I would be ignoring my duty if I let that happen."

Pollyanna sighed. She was beginning to dislike this word "duty."

"Aunt Polly," she said, "do you think that there's any way to be glad about this duty business?"

"Excuse me?" Miss Polly said. "Don't be rude, Pollyanna!" Miss Polly left the attic room without slamming the door.

Pollyanna sat in the chair. She wondered if the rest of her days would be filled with nothing but duty. *I guess there isn't anything to be glad about*, she thought to herself. *Unless, of course, I can be glad when the duty's done!*

Then with that thought, Pollyanna laughed out loud.

CHAPTER 5

Pollyanna Pays a Visit

It wasn't too long before the Harrington home settled into a new routine. It was not the kind of order that Miss Polly was used to, however. Pollyanna did her duties. She cooked, sewed, and worked on her lessons. She did everything Aunt Polly asked. In exchange, Aunt Polly let her have most of the afternoon for "living."

No one in the household knew whether Miss Polly made this deal for Pollyanna's sake or her own. They certainly noticed the many times Miss Polly sighed while sewing with her niece.

Or how often she said, "My word, you are an extraordinary child." It was quite possible that Miss Polly was looking for some peace and quiet in the afternoons.

Pollyanna always asked for errands to run. She enjoyed any opportunity to walk into town to meet new people. It was on these walks that she usually saw the Man.

Pollyanna referred to him as the Man because she did not know his name. He was tall and thin. He looked quite old—although not as old as Tom. He wore a long black coat and a tall silk hat. The Man was always alone— except for his dog. The dog trotted happily behind the Man. Pollyanna noticed that the dog sometimes licked his hand. Even though the Man never smiled at the dog, he always patted his head gently. Pollyanna could tell that the dog and the Man loved each other very much.

One day she said, "How do you do, sir? It's a nice day, isn't it?"

The Man stopped uncertainly. He looked at Pollyanna. "Did you just speak to me?"

"Yes, sir," Pollyanna said. "I just said that it's a nice day."

The Man mumbled something and walked off.

When they passed each other the next day, Pollyanna said hello again. On the third day, he stopped. "Why do you keep saying hello? Who are you?"

"My name is Pollyanna Whittier. I thought you looked a bit lonesome. I'm glad that you finally stopped. I'm afraid I don't know your name."

Once again the Man walked away without another word. Pollyanna wondered if the Man understood her.

She continued on her way to Mrs. Snow's house. Mrs. Snow was stuck in her bed because she could not walk. She had been sick for a very long time.

Millie, her daughter, took care of her. Miss Polly and several other women from the church took turns helping. They usually sent her baskets of food.

On Pollyanna's first visit, Millie led her to a dark bedroom at the back of the house. It took a moment for Pollyanna's eyes to adjust to the light. She noticed the dim outline of a woman sitting up in bed.

"Hello, Mrs. Snow," Pollyanna said. She walked to the side of the bed and held out her hand. "It's a pleasure to meet you. I've brought some jelly from my aunt Polly. I hope you like it. I had some for breakfast this morning and it was delicious."

"Jelly?" Mrs. Snow said. "Oh dear, I suppose that will do. I was really hoping for soup today."

"I thought it was chicken?" Pollyanna asked innocently.

"Pardon me?" Mrs. Snow asked.

"I thought it was chicken that you wanted

when you got jelly. That's what Nancy told me. She said that you usually want chicken when she brings jelly and soup when she brings chicken. But maybe I'm confused. Nancy was muttering when she told me, so I might have mixed things up."

Mrs. Snow sat up straight in bed. This was an unusual thing for Mrs. Snow to do, although Pollyanna did not know that. "Well, Miss Rude, who are you?"

Pollyanna laughed. "Oh, that isn't my name. Wouldn't it be awful if it were? Nancy certainly wouldn't complain about her name if that were mine. My name is Pollyanna Whittier. I am Miss Polly Harrington's niece."

Mrs. Snow relaxed into her pillows again. "That's fine, then. Your aunt was very kind to send the jelly even though I really wanted soup today." Mrs. Snow straightened the sheets on her bed.

"Go to the window, child. Pull the curtains open so that I can see you. I want to know what you look like."

Pollyanna did as she was asked. "I was hoping that you wouldn't have to see my freckles," the girl said. "But at least this means I'll finally be able to see you."

Pollyanna turned back from the window to look at Mrs. Snow. "Good heavens," she said. "No one told me you were so pretty!"

"Pretty?" Mrs. Snow exclaimed. "Me?"

"Why yes!" Pollyanna exclaimed. "Didn't you know it?"

"No, I don't think of such things," Mrs. Snow said dryly.

"Your eyes are so big and dark. And your hair is dark and curly, too. I would love to have hair like yours."

"I haven't spent much time thinking about my looks. Why should I bother when I'm lying on my back in bed all the time?" Mrs. Snow fixed the sheets on her bed again.

"Would you like to look at yourself in the mirror?" Pollyanna asked. "Oh, wait," the girl said. "Let me fix your hair first. I want you to have the full effect when you see yourself."

"I suppose that would be all right," Mrs. Snow said slowly.

"I love fixing people's hair," Pollyanna said. She grabbed a comb and some ribbon from the dresser.

Pollyanna chatted away happily while she worked on Mrs. Snow's hair. The woman grumbled a bit and complained if she pulled too hard. Secretly, though, Mrs. Snow was very pleased with the attention. It had been a long time since anyone had fussed over her. At last Pollyanna was finished. She held up a mirror for Mrs. Snow.

"Now do you see that I am right?" Pollyanna asked. She was very excited. "You look so pretty."

"I don't think those pink ribbons suit me," Mrs. Snow said. "I'm much fonder of red ribbons."

"Well," Pollyanna said as she put things back on the dresser, "I'll have more time the next time I come. We can try different colors then, if you'd like."

Mrs. Snow continued to look at herself in the mirror as she spoke. "I don't see why you'd bother. I'm just going to make a mess of it lying in bed."

"That just means we can fix it up every time I come over," Pollyanna answered. "It was nice to meet you, Mrs. Snow. I really must be going now. Thanks for letting me fix your hair." The girl gave a cheerful wave as she left the room.

When Millie came to check on her mother, she found the drapes open and her mother with ribbons in her hair.

"Mother!" she said. "Your room is so bright!"

"And what if it is?" Mrs. Snow said. "Should I sit in the dark all day just because I'm sick?"

Millie stared at her mother for a few moments. She wondered if she had ever seen her mother look so pretty.

∾

It was a rainy day the next time Pollyanna saw the Man. She said hello to him as they passed on the road, but he did not respond. Pollyanna assumed that he did not hear her.

The next day was bright and sunny. Once again, Pollyanna said hello. The Man responded with a grunt but did not stop.

"How are you?" Pollyanna chirped. "Aren't you glad that it's not yesterday?"

"Pardon me?" the Man said. He stopped walking to look at Pollyanna. "Listen to me, little girl," he said gruffly. "I have much more important things to do than talk about the weather. I don't waste time noticing whether or not the sun shines."

"That's why I mentioned it," Pollyanna said. She smiled brightly at the Man.

"Pardon me?" he asked again.

"It seemed that you didn't pay attention to the sun shining, so I thought I'd mention it to you." Pollyanna put her hands behind her back. She rocked back and forth as she spoke. "I thought it would make you happy if you stopped to notice that the sun was shining."

He shook his head in amazement. "Why don't you find someone your own age to talk to?" he said.

"I would, but there aren't any nearby. Besides, I like talking to older people. It's probably because I spent so much time with the Ladies' Aid."

The Man grunted before walking away.

The next time they met on the road, the Man spoke first. "Before you say anything," he said, "I'll have you know that I already realize the sun is shining."

"I knew that you knew it as soon as I saw you," Pollyanna laughed. "I could see it in your eyes." She looked at him closely. "And your smile."

Once again the Man grunted before walking away.

From that day on, the Man always spoke to Pollyanna. Sometimes, he even spoke first. They rarely said more than "good day," but it was a happy routine.

One day, Nancy noticed Pollyanna walking away from the Man. She ran up to meet Pollyanna.

"Did that man speak to you?" Nancy asked breathlessly.

"Of course," Pollyanna said. "He always speaks to me now."

"Sake's alive! Do you know who that man is?"

Pollyanna shook her head.

"Mr. John Pendleton!" Nancy exclaimed. "He lives in the big house on Pendleton Hill. He's a man of mystery. He lives all on his own. He doesn't even have a cook. Mr. Pendleton walks to the hotel for three meals a day."

"Really?" Pollyanna said. She loved a good mystery.

"He has loads of money. There's no one in town as rich as Mr. Pendleton," Nancy said. "He could eat dollar bills without even noticing."

"That's silly," Pollyanna giggled. "As if anyone wouldn't notice they were chewing on a dollar bill."

"I just mean that he has so many that he wouldn't miss them," Nancy explained. "And he never spends his money on anything. Everyone says he's a very cheap man. Except he goes on trips now and then."

"Oh, you mean he's a missionary," Pollyanna said. Her father knew many missionaries.

"No, not exactly," Nancy said. "I think he writes books about the places he visits. I'm not really sure. He's been all over the world, they say. I've also heard that he has a skeleton in the closet."

"Nancy!" Pollyanna said. She was shocked. "How could you say that about someone?"

"I don't mean it literally," Nancy laughed. "That's what you say when someone has a secret. It's just a saying."

"Well the only thing I know," Pollyanna said, "is that I'm glad he talks to me now. He has the most interesting face, don't you think?"

Nancy shook her head. "I can't say that I've looked too closely," she said. Nancy looked at Pollyanna. The little girl really had a special way of looking at the world.

CHAPTER 6

Miss Polly Visits the Attic Room

∽

One day as Pollyanna walked down from her room, she ran into her aunt on the stairs. "Oh, Aunt Polly!" she exclaimed. "You were just coming up to see me. How lovely! I adore having company." Pollyanna ran back up the stairs and held her door open for her aunt.

Miss Polly did not want to admit that she had been heading to the attic to look for a white shawl. She followed her niece into her room and sat on the chair.

"I'm not used to having company," Pollyanna giggled. "I'm usually the one doing the visiting. I like bringing people things, too. Whenever I bring Mrs. Snow jelly, she says that she wants chicken. Then if I bring her chicken, she says that she wants soup. So Nancy and I decided to bring her all three. When she said that she'd rather have chicken or jelly or soup, she got all of them." Pollyanna laughed. "It was very funny, Aunt Polly. Mrs. Snow didn't say thank you, but I know that she liked it. She smiled a bit more than usual and that says a lot. Don't you think, Aunt Polly?"

Miss Polly did not have time to reply. Pollyanna started on a new topic before her aunt had a chance.

"Although I must say, this isn't the most comfortable room to entertain in," Pollyanna said without thinking. "It's not the room that I planned . . ."

Pollyanna stopped mid-sentence. She realized too late that she was saying something rude. "I'm sorry, Aunt Polly. I didn't mean to say that."

Miss Polly stood up. "Well, you meant to say something. You should finish your thought."

"I only meant," Pollyanna said softly, "I was really looking forward to having a room with a carpet and pictures on the walls. But I don't mind so much anymore. I just play the game that Father taught . . ." Once again Pollyanna stopped in mid-sentence. She remembered that Aunt Polly didn't want her to mention father.

"Honestly, Aunt Polly," she continued. "At first I was sad that I didn't have a mirror. Then I realized that I wouldn't have to look at my freckles, so I didn't mind. And when I saw the beautiful view from my window, I didn't mind not having any pictures on the wall. Oh please, Aunt Polly. You've been so good to me."

"That's enough, Pollyanna," Miss Polly said. "I think you've said your piece." Miss Polly quickly left the room and swept down the stairs. She went straight to the kitchen.

"Nancy," she said quickly. "I want you to move my niece's things to the room directly below hers." She noticed Nancy's surprised look. "I've decided that she should sleep downstairs from now on," Miss Polly said more softly.

A few minutes later, Nancy rushed up to the attic room. She found Pollyanna crying on her bed.

"Why are you crying?" she asked. "Come on! We need to pack your things. We're moving you downstairs."

Pollyanna sat up. "Really? Into that pretty room with the four-poster bed?"

When Nancy said yes, Pollyanna ran downstairs to find her aunt.

"Is it true, Aunt Polly?" Pollyanna was out of breath. "Can I really move downstairs?"

Miss Polly tried not to smile. She thought it would be best to show no emotion. "Yes, you may move to the new room. However, I must have your word that you will be careful in that room. You must not damage the carpet or knock down any pictures."

"I promise, Aunt Polly," the girl said. She clapped her hands and danced on her toes. "And I promise to do my best not to slam doors. I know that you don't like that and I'm always forgetting. I guess I bang doors sometimes when I'm glad about things. And I realize that you're never glad about anything, so you don't need to bang doors. I will do my best, though. I'm sure I'll improve if I set my mind to it."

Pollyanna threw her arms around Miss Polly's neck. She gave her a great big hug. "I'll pack right away. Thank you! Oh, Aunt Polly, I love you so much."

Miss Polly watched Pollyanna run up the stairs. She tried to remember the last time she had been glad about something. There must have been something!

Normally, Miss Polly was very composed. She rarely expressed any kind of emotion. Therefore, she was very surprised to realize that she had tears in her eyes.

CHAPTER 7

Introducing Jimmy

✿

It was mid-August when Pollyanna came home with a stray creature. It was not a dog or cat. It was a little boy in need of a home. Pollyanna was certain that her aunt would allow him to move in with them. How could she say no?

She had met him on the road home from Mrs. Snow's house. Pollyanna was in very good spirits that day. She and Mrs. Snow had been playing the Just Be Glad game all afternoon. Mrs. Snow was finally getting the hang of it. So

Pollyanna was happily skipping along when she saw a boy sitting on a rock.

He was tossing stones into a hat on the ground. Pollyanna sat down beside him. Although she often said she did not mind having no other children to play with, she did feel lonely sometimes. Therefore, she decided to make the most of this situation.

"How are you?" Pollyanna asked brightly.

"Fine," the boy mumbled.

"My name is Pollyanna Whittier. What's yours?"

The boy looked like he was about to run away. He looked shyly at Pollyanna and said, "Jimmy Bean."

"Good. Now that we know each other's names, we can be friends." Pollyanna smiled at Jimmy. "I live at Miss Polly Harrington's house. Where do you live?"

"Nowhere," Jimmy said sadly.

"Nowhere?" Pollyanna exclaimed. "How is that possible?"

"What I mean is," Jimmy said slowly, "I'm just hunting for a new place."

"What kind of place are you looking for?" Pollyanna asked.

The boy gave her a quizzical look. "You sure do ask a lot of questions," he said.

"Well how else am I going to find out anything about you," she asked. "I wouldn't talk so much if you would talk more."

Jimmy laughed. "I suppose so," he said. He stopped tossing stones and faced Pollyanna. "All right, then. Here goes. I'm Jimmy Bean and I'm almost eleven years old. I came to live at the Orphans' Home last year, but there are too many kids there, and they don't want me. At least I know that there isn't enough room for all of us. So I've decided to find someplace else to live. I've gone to four houses already, and they all said no. I told them I'd work to earn my keep, but they still said no."

"Why don't you come and live with my Aunt Polly?" Pollyanna said brightly. "She took me in when my father died. She's very kind and generous, even though she likes to pretend that she isn't. I'm sure she'll let you stay with us."

Pollyanna was so excited that she grabbed Jimmy's hand and practically pulled him down the road.

"Do you really think your aunt will keep me?" Jimmy asked, amazed. "I promise to work real hard. And I don't eat much!"

"Oh, don't worry about Aunt Polly," Pollyanna said. As they ran down the road, she told Jimmy all about her life. She told him about her father, the Ladies' Aid, and coming to live with Aunt Polly. "You might have to sleep in the attic room," she said. "I did at first. But there are screens now, so it won't be so hot. Since you have freckles—just like me—you won't mind that there's no mirror. And the view from the windows is beautiful."

"Gosh," Jimmy exclaimed. He was out of breath from running. "I didn't know anyone could talk so much while running."

Pollyanna laughed. "Oh, there are lots of things you don't know about me."

When they arrived at the house, Pollyanna brought Jimmy straight to the living room. Miss Polly was sitting in her chair, sewing. She looked up when the children entered.

"Aunt Polly, this is Jimmy Bean," the girl said. "He lives in the Orphans' Home, but there's not enough room for him. I told him that he could live here, and you'd bring him up alongside me. He's willing to work and doesn't ask for much, so there's nothing to worry about."

Miss Polly's face first went white and then red. "What is the meaning of this? Why did you bring this dirty little boy here?"

When Jimmy heard the words "dirty little boy," he took a couple of steps back. He hung his head slightly. He was embarrassed about being dirty.

"Why, Aunt Polly," Pollyanna exclaimed. "I just told you that he's from—"

"Pollyanna," her aunt interrupted. "I heard what you said. I just don't understand why you thought to bring him here."

"But there are so many rooms in the house," the girl said. She really did not understand her aunt. This seemed like such a simple solution.

There was a stirring in the hallway as Jimmy stepped forward. "I'm not a beggar, ma'am," he said. He held his head high. "Just because I'm an orphan and want to have a home doesn't mean that I'm begging for anything. I plan to work for my keep wherever I go. The only reason I came here was because Pollyanna kept saying that you were good and kind. Well you can keep your empty rooms and big house! I don't need them."

Jimmy quickly ran out of the house.

Pollyanna stared. "But Aunt Polly," she said. "I thought you would be glad to help—"

"Glad?" Miss Polly interrupted. "Pollyanna, would you please stop using that word! I am so sick of hearing you say *glad* this and *glad* that. It's infuriating!"

"I'm sorry, Aunt Polly," she said. "I just thought you'd be gl—" Before she could finish the word, Pollyanna clapped a hand over her mouth. Rather than say anything else, she turned and ran out of the house after Jimmy.

She finally caught up with him at the end of the driveway. "Jimmy," she called. "Please wait! I'm so sorry."

He stopped. "I don't blame you," he said gruffly. "I guess I'm just disappointed. I had my hopes up."

"You must believe me," she said breathlessly, "Aunt Polly is very kind and generous. She took me in when I didn't have anywhere else to go. I probably didn't explain it to her right."

"Don't worry about it," Jimmy said. He turned to walk back down the road.

"Wait," Pollyanna called. "I still want to find you a place to live. You deserve as nice a home as I've got."

The two children walked down the road in silence for a few minutes. Pollyanna did not see her aunt watching them from the window. Miss Polly sighed and walked upstairs. She could still hear the little boy calling her "good and kind." Deep in her heart, Miss Polly felt very sad. Although she couldn't explain it, she felt like she had lost something.

CHAPTER 8

In Pendleton Woods

⌒

After she and Jimmy parted ways, Pollyanna headed toward Pendleton Woods. Even Pollyanna had to admit that it was a tough day. She still felt disappointed that her aunt wouldn't take Jimmy Bean. She thought a nice quiet walk through the woods would clear her head.

Suddenly she heard a dog barking. It sounded quite frantic. A moment later the dog came bounding through the woods, almost knocking her over. She recognized the dog. It belonged to Mr. Pendleton.

"Here, doggie," Pollyanna called. She snapped her fingers. "Come here, boy." She hoped that Mr. Pendleton was close behind.

The dog, however, was acting strangely. It raced part of the way back into the woods, then came back to Pollyanna. It did this a few more times while barking.

"Where are you going, doggie?" Pollyanna asked. "That's not the way home." After a few moments, she understood that the dog wanted her to follow. So she did.

Not far down the path, Pollyanna discovered the reason for the dog's barking. Mr. Pendleton was lying on the ground.

"Oh, Mr. Pendleton!" she cried. "Are you hurt?"

He turned to look at Pollyanna as she rushed to his side.

"Hurt? No, of course not. I'm just taking a late afternoon nap in the woods," he snapped.

"Don't you have any sense? Why would you ask a silly question like that?"

Pollyanna gasped. She was shocked by his tone. As usual, though, she answered his questions honestly.

"Sense? Well, I don't know if I have any sense. Most of the Ladies' Aid—except Mrs. Patterson—thought I had a great deal of sense."

Mr. Pendleton shook his head. "I'm sorry, child. I shouldn't have spoken to you that way. It's this darn leg of mine. I'm in a terrible amount of pain."

"What can I do to help?" Pollyanna asked. She was very concerned about Mr. Pendleton.

The man reached into his pocket and pulled out a key. "Take this. Run down the path. You'll see my house in a few minutes. Use this key to open the side door. Do you know how to use a telephone?"

"Yes, Mr. Pendleton," Pollyanna responded. "I've only done it once, but I've seen Aunt Polly do it plenty of times."

"Good. Look beside the phone and you'll find a list of numbers. Call Dr. Chilton. Tell him to bring men and a stretcher and come here immediately. Tell him that Mr. Pendleton has a broken leg."

"A broken leg!?" Pollyanna exclaimed. "How awful! Whatever can I do to help?"

"You can telephone the doctor," Mr. Pendleton sighed.

"Would you like me to build you a pillow so you're more comfortable?" Pollyanna looked about her for leaves or grass.

"Why do you punish me like this?" Mr. Pendleton cried. "Why can't you just go call the doctor? That's what I need."

Pollyanna jumped up and said that she'd be back soon. Then she ran toward the house.

In a few short minutes she was back at Mr. Pendleton's side with a blanket.

"What? Why have you come back so soon?" Mr. Pendleton said. He looked very worried and in pain. "Did you have trouble getting into the house?"

"Of course I got inside the house," Pollyanna said. "Where else would I find a blanket?" She laughed at Mr. Pendleton's question. "I've already called the doctor, and he said he would be here shortly. He said that he knew exactly where you were, so I didn't bother waiting for him. I thought it would be better if I kept you company instead. I wanted to be with you."

"You did," the man said, amazed. "Well, I can't say that I admire your taste. I would think you could find more pleasant companions."

"Do you mean because you're so cross?" Pollyanna asked.

"Thank you for your frankness. Yes, because I

am so cross," Mr. Pendleton tried not to smile.

"Oh, you're only cross on the outside. You're not cross on the inside one bit."

"And how do you know that?" Mr. Pendleton asked.

"Lots of ways," Pollyanna said. "For instance, the way you are with your dog. You can fool lots of people, but you can't fool animals. They can see folk's insides a lot better than people can."

Pollyanna looked at Mr. Pendleton. The poor man was clearly in a lot of pain. She wanted to help him as best she could. "I'm going to hold your hand if that's all right, Mr. Pendleton," she said.

The man started to object. However, as soon as Pollyanna took his hand he felt calmer. They waited together in the woods until the doctor and his men arrived.

Dr. Chilton, a tall handsome man, walked

quickly through the woods. He smiled when he saw Pollyanna holding the old man's hand. "Well, my little lady, playing nurse?" he said.

"Oh no, sir," she replied. "I've only been holding his hand. I haven't given him one bit of medicine."

The doctor laughed. "Don't worry," he said. "I'm sure you've done nothing wrong."

"I'm just glad I was here," Pollyanna added.

"So am I," Dr. Chilton replied.

CHAPTER 9

Just a Matter of Jelly

∽

Pollyanna could not tell her aunt about Mr. Pendleton's accident because Miss Polly was called away suddenly. A cousin in Boston had died, so Miss Polly caught the next train. Pollyanna shared her story with Nancy, of course, and anyone else who might listen. Miss Polly found out when she returned a week later. They were having breakfast when Pollyanna brought up the subject.

"Aunt Polly," she asked, "would you mind terribly if I took Mrs. Snow's jelly to someone else today? I know that Mrs. Snow wants the jelly and that she likes having visitors, but Mrs. Snow is always going to be in that bed. People with broken legs aren't like lifelong invalids. His broken leg won't last forever, so I think I should take him the jelly instead."

"Oh, child," Miss Polly sighed. Why did this child have to be so tiring first thing in the morning? "Whatever are you talking about? Who is this 'He'? What broken leg are you talking about?"

"Oh, I forgot!" Pollyanna said. "You haven't heard anything about this!" So Pollyanna told her aunt the story of walking through the woods and finding the man.

"That was very good of you, Pollyanna," her aunt said. "You fulfilled your duty very well. Who did you say this man was?"

"I don't think I did," Pollyanna answered. "It was Mr. John Pendleton."

"John Pendleton!" Miss Polly exclaimed.

"Yes," the girl said. "Do you know him?"

Her aunt did not answer her. Instead, she asked another question. "Do *you* know him?"

Pollyanna nodded. "Yes. He always says hello to me now. At least he did. Now, of course, he's lying in bed with a broken leg. That's why I want to take him the jelly. I'm sure he's all alone. He's so cross on the outside that most people don't pay him much attention. I know that he's not cross on the inside but most other people don't see that. I'm worried that he's all by himself—except when Dr. Chilton comes to visit."

"D-D-Dr. Chilton?" Miss Polly stuttered. "Did you meet Dr. Chilton, as well?"

"Yes, that's who I called on the telephone." Pollyanna did not notice that all the color had drained from her aunt's face.

"He is a very nice and handsome man," Pollyanna added. "He even called me a little nurse because I was holding Mr. Pendleton's hand when the men arrived."

"Does Mr. Pendleton—or Dr. Chilton—know that I am your aunt?" Miss Polly asked softly.

"No, I reckon not," Pollyanna said. "I told them my name, but I didn't say where I lived."

The two sat quietly at the table for a few minutes. Finally, Miss Polly cleared her throat to speak.

"Very well, Pollyanna," she said. "You may take the jelly to Mr. Pendleton. Just remember that it is a gift from you. I did not send it. Please make sure that he doesn't think that I did."

"Thank you, Aunt Polly." The girl hugged her aunt. "I promise."

She ran out the door with the jar of jelly in her hand.

Mr. Pendleton's house looked very different this time. All the windows were open. There was an old woman hanging up clothes in the backyard.

Pollyanna went to the side door and rang the doorbell. She had to wait a few minutes for the old woman to come in from the yard to answer the door. The woman looked at Pollyanna with curiosity. She clearly did not expect a young girl to arrive.

"Good morning," Pollyanna said brightly. "I've come to see Mr. Pendleton. And I've brought him some jelly."

"Who shall I say brought the jelly?" the woman asked.

Dr. Chilton walked into the hall at that moment. He saw Pollyanna at the door and smiled broadly.

"Well, if it's not our little nurse," he said. "Have you met Mrs. Johnson? She is here to help Mr. Pendleton while his leg heals. Why don't you come in? Maybe you would like to see our patient?"

Mrs. Johnson looked confused. "But Mr.

Pendleton said he wanted absolutely no visitors," she whispered to the doctor.

"This visit is under doctor's orders," he replied. "I believe Miss Pollyanna has exactly the tonic Mr. Pendleton needs."

"Thank you, Dr. Chilton," Pollyanna said. "I've been looking forward to seeing Mr. Pendleton all morning."

After Pollyanna was sent down the hall, the old woman turned to Dr. Chilton. "Who is that girl? I don't believe I've seen her before."

"Ah, you don't know the marvelous Miss Pollyanna Whittier? She is a young girl of extraordinary powers. I can't pinpoint it exactly, but I think her secret is an overwhelming, endless sense of gladness. She's already come in contact with many of my patients, so I'm familiar with her work. There appears to be something that she refers to as the Just Be Glad game. It has had an incredible effect on people. Men and women who barely noticed that the sun was shining can now talk for twenty minutes about its perfect color. It's astonishing, really. I don't know why someone didn't think of it sooner."

Pollyanna, meanwhile, was making her way down a long hallway. She passed by a large, rather dark dining room. She quickly looked inside the library. The walls were filled top to bottom with books. A tall ladder was attached to the shelves so Mr. Pendleton could reach the books at the top.

She knocked on Mr. Pendleton's door.

"What do you want?" a gruff voice said. "I thought I told you I didn't want any visitors!"

Pollyanna opened the door slowly. "Good morning, Mr. Pendleton," she called. "I stopped by to see how you were feeling and bring you some jelly."

"Jelly?" he asked. "Never eat it!" Then he saw Pollyanna walk into the room. "Ah, it's you.

Well, I guess it's all right if you come in for a bit."

"The jelly was supposed to go to Mrs. Snow, but I thought it might be nicer if you had it. You've got a broken leg—and broken legs don't last forever—so I thought you might need a bit of jelly and company. Mrs. Snow is a lifelong invalid, so there'll be plenty of time to bring her jelly. That sounds a bit mean, doesn't it? I didn't mean it that way. I only meant that Mrs. Snow is used to being in bed. It's not pleasant for her, but it's the life that she knows. You, on the other hand, are used to walking every day. So I thought the jelly might be more useful here."

"You've put an awful lot of thought into this, haven't you?" Mr. Pendleton smiled slightly.

Pollyanna laughed at herself. "I do sometimes think myself into circles."

Mr. Pendleton laughed, too. He tried to return to his grumpy look but it was too late. Pollyanna knew that she had made him laugh.

"I think that you should learn how to play the Just Be Glad game," Pollyanna said. "You'd be quite good at it, even though you try to be the grumpiest man in town."

"I don't like games," he said. "Games are for children."

Pollyanna ignored his comments and continued talking.

"My father taught me the game. No matter what happens to you—no matter how bad it may seem—you just need to find something that makes you glad. For instance, you should be glad that a broken leg doesn't last forever. When my father went to heaven, I was glad that I finally got to meet my aunt Polly. So you see, even something as sad as that can have something good."

"Polly?" Mr. Pendleton interrupted her. "Did you say 'Aunt Polly?'"

"Yes," Pollyanna said. "When my father died I moved here to live with my aunt Polly."

"What did you say your name was?" Mr. Pendleton was trying to sit up in bed. He was clearly in distress.

"My name is Pollyanna Whittier. My aunt's name is Miss Polly Harrington."

Mr. Pendleton's face grew red with anger. "Am I to understand that Polly Harrington sent me jelly?"

"Oh no," Pollyanna cried. "The jelly is from me. It was entirely my idea. As a matter of fact, Aunt Polly wanted you to know that the jelly most definitely did not come from her. She said so very clearly."

"I thought as much," he said and closed his eyes. He turned his head away.

Poor Pollyanna did not know what to do. She hoped that Mr. Pendleton was sleeping. It would be awful to think that he did not want to talk to her. Pollyanna tiptoed out of the room and softly closed the door behind her.

Dr. Chilton was waiting on the front porch as Pollyanna left the house. "May I offer you a ride home, Miss Whittier?"

She thanked him kindly and stepped into his buggy. It was a pleasant ride. Dr. Chilton was a kind man who enjoyed listening to Pollyanna. The little girl was enjoying herself very much, although she did feel a bit sorry for the doctor. Sometimes she looked at him and he looked so sad. She wondered what he was thinking about.

"You know, Dr. Chilton," she said, "I think being a doctor must be the gladdest job in the world."

"Glad?" he said. "When I have to see people that are sick or hurt?"

"But you are helping people," she said. "It must feel wonderful knowing that you are making a difference."

Dr. Chilton smiled at the little girl. She was working her magic on him, as well. The next time he thought his day was too long or too hard, he would think of her words.

"I suppose I could say the same thing to you, Miss Pollyanna," the doctor said. "You've made quite a difference in people's lives, too."

Pollyanna smiled. "It's all just a part of living," she said. "What's the point of feeling glad if you can't share it with someone?"

The buggy pulled into Miss Polly's yard, and Pollyanna climbed down. She waved a hearty good-bye to Dr. Chilton and went inside. She found her Aunt Polly in the living room. Her aunt was pacing across the room.

"Who was that man who brought you home?" she asked sharply.

"It was Dr. Chilton," Pollyanna answered. "Don't you know him?"

"Dr. Chilton! What on earth was he doing here?" Miss Polly exclaimed.

"I took the jelly to Mr. Pendleton and Dr.

Chilton drove me home," the girl answered. She wondered why her aunt was so upset.

"Does Mr. Pendleton think the jelly came from me?" Miss Polly asked.

"No, I made sure to tell him that it did not come from you."

"Excuse me? You *TOLD* him that I did not send it?" Miss Polly was furious.

"B-but, Aunt Polly, you told me to say that," Pollyanna stuttered.

"I did nothing of the kind. I didn't want him to think that I sent it, which is very different than telling him that I did not send it."

Pollyanna looked at her aunt. She felt very confused at that moment. "Dear me! Well, I don't see what the difference is."

Pollyanna left the living room. She hung her coat in the hall and went up to her room. She wondered if she would ever understand adults.

CHAPTER 10

A Red Rose and a Lace Shawl

෮

A week later Miss Polly returned from a Ladies' Aid meeting with very windswept hair. It was a breezy day. The buggy had loosened the pins in her hair. Curls were falling down around her face. Her black hair looked wild and messy.

When Pollyanna saw her aunt, she squealed, "Aunt Polly! You look so pretty!" Pollyanna clapped her hands with joy. "I had no idea your hair was so lovely. It's always pinned back so tightly. Why don't you wear it loose more often?"

"My goodness, what are you talking about?" Miss Polly said. She looked at herself in the hall mirror. "Why would you say that I look pretty? I look awful. My hair is a complete mess."

Miss Polly did not want to admit it but she liked hearing Pollyanna's comments. She couldn't remember the last time someone cared how her hair looked. It had been a very long time.

"Aunt Polly," Pollyanna said, "may I please do your hair?" Pollyanna danced on her tiptoes in front of her aunt.

"I've had a very hard day, Pollyanna. I've been talking all morning with the ladies at the meeting . . ."

"Aha!" Pollyanna exclaimed. "You didn't say that I couldn't do your hair. It's just like with Mr. Pendleton's jelly. I got confused last time but I think I understand now. It's what you *don't* say that matters. Right?"

Miss Polly stared at her niece. She did not know how to respond.

"Wait right where you are! I'll go get a comb." Pollyanna ran off to get supplies.

Before Miss Polly knew it, she was sitting in front of her dressing mirror while Pollyanna fixed her hair. The girl used ribbons and pins to create full pretty curls. Even Miss Polly was amazed. She really did look different. She had to admit that she almost felt pretty.

"Wait one second," Pollyanna said. "I have the perfect finishing touch." She ran out of the room. When she returned, she was carrying a white lace shawl. "I'll wrap this around your shoulders. I think it's the perfect touch of elegance."

"Oh, Pollyanna," Miss Polly scoffed. "Don't be so silly. I'm not one for playing dress-up."

"Come with me," Pollyanna said. She ignored her aunt's objections. "I want you to come into the sunroom so I can see you better. There's much more light there."

Miss Polly let herself be led into the other room. Pollyanna brought along a hand mirror. Just before Miss Polly looked into the mirror, Pollyanna placed a single rose behind her aunt's ear.

"Oh, Aunt Polly," she said. "You look wonderful."

For a few moments, Miss Polly stared at herself in the mirror. She was overcome by a strange emotion. It had been a long time since she had felt anything like it. Then she heard something outside and looked into the yard. She let out a short cry and ran from the room.

Pollyanna looked outside and saw a buggy. She instantly recognized the man holding the reins. It was Dr. Chilton. She ran to tell Aunt Polly that they had a visitor.

"Aunt Polly," she called. "Dr. Chilton is here!"

Pollyanna ran into her aunt's bedroom. Miss Polly was sitting at her mirror, pulling out all the ribbons and pins. Her aunt was red faced and looked like she was about to cry.

"How dare you do this to me," Miss Polly said. "You've made me look like a fool."

"No, Aunt Polly," Pollyanna said. "You look beautiful. I don't see why you're getting so upset."

"Of course you wouldn't," Aunt Polly snapped. "That's because you only think of yourself. You dressed me up like this, then let me be seen!"

"But Aunt Polly," Pollyanna sobbed. "You look so pretty. Please leave your hair up for a little while longer."

"Please, Pollyanna," her aunt said. She held her head in her hands. "I need to be alone right now."

"Okay," Pollyanna said softly. She fought back tears as she backed out of the room.

Pollyanna went outside to find Dr. Chilton waiting for her.

"I wondered when you were going to come outside," he said cheerfully. "I was starting to worry that I would have to ring the doorbell."

"I'm sorry, Dr. Chilton," Pollyanna said. "I was just talking to Aunt Polly."

"Yes, of course," Dr. Chilton said. He cleared his throat. "I've come to collect you. One of my patients needs you."

"Do you need me to run an errand?" Pollyanna asked.

"No, I need you to come for a visit. Mr. Pendleton could use a bit of your company. Do you think your aunt could spare you for a few hours?"

Pollyanna looked back at the house. "Yes," she said rather softly. "I think Aunt Polly would be very happy if I weren't around."

"Is everything all right, Pollyanna?" the doctor asked. "Is your aunt all right? I thought I saw her in the window as I was driving up the lane."

"Yes, she's fine." Pollyanna hung her head. "She's just a bit mad at me. I fixed up her hair, and she looked so beautiful. Then she suddenly became very upset and said I made her look foolish."

"I'm sorry, Pollyanna," he said.

"I think it had something to do with you," she looked up at the doctor. "She looked into the yard and saw you pull up. Then she ran off and accused me of dressing her up like a fool."

"I'm sure she didn't mean what she said," he added.

"And she did look pretty, Dr. Chilton," Pollyanna said.

"I'm sure she did," the doctor answered. "I have no doubt that she did."

CHAPTER 11

A Question Answered

ᥫᨒ

Mr. Pendleton greeted Pollyanna with a smile. "You must be a very forgiving person," he said. "I was so rude to you last time that I was worried you wouldn't come back."

"Why, I was glad to come," Pollyanna said. "Why wouldn't I?"

"I was cross with you last time. And I was cross that time you found me in the woods. I don't think I've ever thanked you for that," Mr. Pendleton said. "You were very brave."

Pollyanna was surprised by the compliment.

She was not sure how to respond. "I'm glad," she said. "I don't mean that I'm glad your leg was broken, of course."

Mr. Pendleton smiled. "No, of course not. Your tongue does get away from you sometimes, doesn't it, Miss Pollyanna?"

She laughed. "Yes, I suppose so."

"I'd like to thank you for the jelly, too," Mr. Pendleton added.

"Did you like it?" Pollyanna asked brightly.

"Yes, very much so," he said.

Pollyanna frowned. "I'm sorry, too," she said. "I was rude when I said that Aunt Polly didn't send the jelly."

Mr. Pendleton did not respond. He looked straight ahead with a very serious expression. Pollyanna worried that she had offended him.

After a few moments, he looked at the little girl again. He smiled, although Pollyanna knew it was forced. She appreciated the effort, though.

"Enough of this moping around, Miss Pollyanna," he said. "That's not why I asked you here today. Go into the library. On the bottom shelf, you'll find a black box with handles. Pick it up and bring it in here. I don't think it will be too heavy for you."

"Oh, I'm very strong," Pollyanna said. She was back in the room in a few minutes with the box.

The next half hour was wonderful! The box was full of treasures that Mr. Pendleton had brought back from his travels. There were figurines from China and a brooch from India. There was a beautifully carved chess set from Nepal. Pollyanna had never seen anything like them! Mr. Pendleton told her marvelous stories about each one.

"I've never seen anything from India before," Pollyanna said wistfully. "I've certainly heard about the missions in India. All of the Ladies' Aids send money to the missions there."

Mr. Pendleton did not hear Pollyanna. He was already holding another treasure from the box and getting set to tell the next tale.

It was a wonderful afternoon. Pollyanna realized that they were talking about much more than the treasures in the box. They were talking about their lives. Pollyanna told him all about Nancy and Aunt Polly and her daily life. She even told him about her life out west before she came to Beldingsville.

When it was time to go, Mr. Pendleton smiled sweetly at Pollyanna. "Promise me that you'll come to visit me often," he said. "I'm a lonely old man and could use the company. You know, you remind me of someone. For a short while I didn't want to see you because the memory was painful. Every day the doctor asked if he should bring you here and I always said no. But then I started to miss you. I wanted to see your bright smile and hear your constant chatter." He looked at Pollyanna and sighed. "And so I'm asking you to come and visit me often. Brighten up an old man's dreary day."

"Of course," Pollyanna said. She felt as if she might cry. "I'll come as often as I can."

That night after dinner, Nancy and Pollyanna sat on the back porch talking. Pollyanna told her friend all about Mr. Pendleton's box of treasures. She tried to describe each piece perfectly.

"When I was leaving," Pollyanna said, "he asked me to come visit him whenever I could. I said yes, of course. I truly enjoy spending time with Mr. Pendleton. But he did say one strange thing. He told me that I remind him of someone. He said that he thought about never seeing me again because it was too painful. Isn't that strange and so sad?"

"You remind him of someone?" Nancy said. She thought about this carefully for a few moments. Suddenly, her eyes went wide with excitement. "My word! Pollyanna, do you know what this means?" Nancy stood up and clapped her hands together.

"Whatever are you talking about?" Pollyanna asked, confused.

"The Mystery!" Nancy crouched down beside Pollyanna. "Now, tell me, was it just after Mr. Pendleton discovered you were Miss Polly's niece that he didn't want to see you?"

"Why, yes," Pollyanna said. "That's exactly when it happened."

"Then, don't you see? Mr. Pendleton used to be Miss Polly's boyfriend!" Nancy was very pleased with herself. She stood up and crossed her arms over her chest.

"Mr. Pendleton? That's impossible!" Pollyanna could not believe her ears.

"But it's true. Old Tom told me himself," Nancy continued. She could not help smiling. "Well, he didn't say who it was, but he did tell me that Miss Polly had a lost love. He said they had a fight and haven't spoken in years. So you see, it all adds up. Mr. Pendleton loved Miss Polly and now you remind him of her."

"I guess he did act pretty strangely about the jelly," Pollyanna said thoughtfully. "But Miss Polly doesn't even like him."

"Of course not!" Nancy exclaimed. "That's because of the fight."

Pollyanna thought things over for a few moments. "I suppose that if they loved each other before, they might do so again. They've both been alone all these years. I would think they'd be happy to make up."

"I guess you don't know much about being in love," Nancy chuckled. "Things are never that easy."

Pollyanna did not respond. When she went into the house a little later, she was very thoughtful.

CHAPTER 12

Prisms

⌒

Pollyanna did as she promised and went to see Mr. Pendleton often. She enjoyed her visits and loved hearing his stories of the world. But she did wonder if she was helping him at all. He didn't seem any less cross having her there. She tried to teach him the Just Be Glad game, but it was never the right time. Whenever she brought up the subject of playing the game with her father, Mr. Pendleton quickly changed the subject.

Pollyanna never doubted that Mr. Pendleton was Miss Polly's onetime love. More than anything else in the world, she wanted to bring both of them happiness.

She often talked to Mr. Pendleton about her aunt. He sometimes listened politely. Other times he angrily changed the subject. Her aunt reacted in the same way whenever Pollyanna brought up the subject of Mr. Pendleton. She was certain this proved that they still had feelings for each other.

Pollyanna noticed that there were some people her aunt did not like discussing. She already knew not to mention her father around Aunt Polly. Her aunt was also very uncomfortable whenever Pollyanna mentioned Dr. Chilton. Pollyanna assumed this was because he had seen her aunt with ribbons in her hair.

One night Pollyanna was feeling feverish. Miss Polly felt her forehead with the back of her hand. "If you start to feel any worse," her aunt said, "we'll have to call the doctor."

"Will we?" Pollyanna said. She was very excited. "Oh, I would love to see Dr. Chilton."

Miss Polly looked sternly at Pollyanna. "Dr. Chilton is not our doctor. We will call Dr. Warren if you feel worse."

"Oh." Pollyanna looked upset. "I don't think I would like that very much. And I don't think Dr. Chilton would either. He really is lovely, you know. It wasn't his fault that he saw you with ribbons in your hair."

"That is enough, Pollyanna!" Miss Polly said crossly. "I will check on you in an hour. We will call Dr. Warren then, if necessary." Miss Polly turned and left the room.

Pollyanna did not feel any worse. They did not call Dr. Warren.

∽

One day Pollyanna noticed a colored light on Mr. Pendleton's wall. "Look at that!" she exclaimed.

"It's a little baby rainbow on your wall. Wherever did that come from?"

"From the sun shining through the window, of course," Mr. Pendleton said. Pollyanna looked at him quizzically. "Surely you've seen a prism before?" he asked.

"I've never even heard the word *prism* before," Pollyanna said matter-of-factly.

"What do they teach you at school?" he said sharply.

"I don't start school here until next month," Pollyanna replied. "I guess we didn't talk about

prisms at my old school."

"When the sunlight goes through the angled glass of that thermometer, it turns the light into a rainbow," he said. He thought about explaining it further but realized he did not know how a prism worked.

"It's so beautiful," she said. "I wish I had one of my own. Wouldn't it be lovely if we could all have a baby rainbow to call our own? I would wish one for Mrs. Snow, too, and Aunt Polly. I think I would like it best if Aunt Polly had one. How could she be anything but glad if she had her own rainbow?"

Mr. Pendleton laughed. "From my experience with your aunt," he said, "it will take more than a few prisms of light to make her glad."

"Oh, I forgot," Pollyanna said. "You don't know about the game."

"The game?" Mr. Pendleton asked.

So Pollyanna told him all about the game, from beginning to end. She did not look at him while talking, though. She could not take her eyes off the baby rainbow. It shimmered against the wall. She felt very glad and content watching the colors and telling Mr. Pendleton about the game.

When she was finished Mr. Pendleton sighed. "You know, Miss Pollyanna, I think the greatest, most wonderful prism of them all is you."

"Oh, but I don't show beautiful red and green and purple when the sun shines through me!" she said.

"Don't you?" the man said, smiling.

Pollyanna wondered why there were tears in his eyes.

"No," she said. "The sun doesn't shine through me. The sun doesn't make anything but freckles. At least that's what Aunt Polly says."

The man laughed a little. Again, Pollyanna looked at him. The laugh sounded almost like a sob.

CHAPTER 13

Another Question Answered

సా

One Saturday afternoon Mr. Pendleton asked Pollyanna a very important question. "How would you like to come and live here?" he asked.

"Mr. Pendleton, you don't really mean that, do you?" she asked.

"Of course, I do," he said. "I think it would be wonderful for both of us."

"But Mr. Pendleton, I can't," she said. "I'm Aunt Polly's."

"You're no more hers than—Perhaps she would let you come to me," he finished more gently. "Would you come if she did?"

Pollyanna frowned in deep thought.

"But Aunt Polly has been so good to me," she said slowly. "And she took me in when I didn't have anybody left but the Ladies' Aid."

It was Mr. Pendleton's turn to frown. When he spoke, his voice was low and very sad. "Pollyanna, many years ago I loved somebody very much. I hoped to bring her to this house. I pictured how happy we'd be together here in our home for all the years to come."

"Yes," Pollyanna said. Her eyes were shining with sympathy.

"When it didn't work out—when she didn't come here—this house has only been a great gray pile of stones. It has never been a home. It takes a woman's hand and heart, or a child's presence, to make a home. I have not had either. Now, will you come and live with me?"

Pollyanna sprang to her feet. Her face was bright and happy.

"Mr. Pendleton, you mean that you wish you had had that woman's hand and heart all along?"

"Why, y-yes, Pollyanna."

"Oh, I'm so glad. Then it's all right," she sighed. "Now you can take us both and everything will be lovely."

"Take you both?" Mr. Pendleton was very confused.

"Aunt Polly and me, of course," Pollyanna said. She danced around the room.

"Aunt Polly?" Mr. Pendleton said. He sounded very shocked, almost cross. "Why would your Aunt Polly come to live here?"

"Because you love her, of course." Pollyanna giggled. "Because you've been waiting for her all these years!"

"You think that I loved your Aunt Polly?" Poor Mr. Pendleton looked like he did not know whether he should laugh or cry.

"Is there something wrong, Mr. Pendleton?" Pollyanna asked.

"I think there's been a misunderstanding," he said. "Please have a seat. Let me explain something to you."

Pollyanna sat in a chair opposite Mr. Pendleton. She waited patiently for him to speak.

"The person who I loved very much was your mother. She did not return my love. She married your father and moved away. I was heartbroken. I returned to this house and locked myself up. I lived here entirely on my own. I went on trips around the world on my own. I did not allow myself to care or to love anyone. Until I met you. You have brought so much sunshine into my life."

"Then why do you and Aunt Polly dislike each other so much?" Pollyanna asked. "Nancy told me you had a lover's fight."

"Nancy? What would she know about this?" Mr. Pendleton shook his head. "I was very angry when your mother rejected me. Your aunt and I fought about it. We said many terrible things to one another and have not spoken for many years. It seems silly now, but it's an old fight. I guess neither of us has tried to apologize."

He looked at Pollyanna. "Will you come to live with me? It will make me very happy."

Pollyanna thought about everything that Mr. Pendleton had said. She thought about Aunt Polly and how much she hated it when doors were slammed. Her aunt was often cross with her for talking too much or running through the house. Then she thought about Mr. Pendleton. He liked her glad game and encouraged her to ask lots of questions.

"Well, Pollyanna," Mr. Pendleton said. "What do you say?"

"I can't do it," she said. "I'm very sorry, but I know that Aunt Polly needs me. She doesn't always act like it, but I know that she does."

Mr. Pendleton looked very sad. "I'm sorry to hear that, Pollyanna," he said. His face went white as he sat back in his chair. "That makes me very sad, indeed." He closed his eyes.

Just then Dr. Chilton walked into the room. He looked at his patient and realized right away that Mr. Pendleton was in need of a rest.

"Pollyanna, I think our patient has had enough of your medicine for the day," he said. "How about I give you a ride home?"

"Thank you, Dr. Chilton," she said. Pollyanna turned to Mr. Pendleton before leaving. "When I come back tomorrow, remind me to tell you about my friend Jimmy Bean."

CHAPTER 14

The Accident

෴

It was late October when the accident occurred. Pollyanna thought she could run across the street before the motorcar reached her. She realized her mistake too late.

No one was sure what happened. People on the street heard Pollyanna cry out and then they heard a crash. Everyone quickly ran to her side. The little girl was in pain and crying.

Pollyanna was carefully placed on a stretcher and rushed home. As soon as Nancy saw her, she began to cry.

"Oh, our poor Pollyanna," she wept. "Will she be all right? Please take her upstairs. I'll get Miss Polly. She's out in the garden."

For the first time in many years, Miss Polly ran. She rushed to her niece's side. The little girl was already unconscious. Her face was white and she looked very, very tired.

"Oh dear, oh dear," Miss Polly cried. "My poor Pollyanna!" Miss Polly's face was wet with tears. She did not stop to wonder why she was crying. She did not think about the fact that she had not cried in years. The only thing she knew was that her niece—whom she loved so much—was hurt.

"Nancy!" she called over her shoulder. "Please send for Dr. Warren."

"I've already telephoned him," Nancy replied.

Miss Polly took Nancy's hand and held it tightly. "We must be very strong for our little girl," she said. "When Pollyanna wakes up, we must be bright and happy—glad—so that she will feel better."

"Y-yes, ma'am," Nancy stuttered. The two women wept beside Pollyanna's bed until the doctor arrived.

Dr. Warren did not have good news for them.

"I won't know for sure until she wakes up," he said, "but I worry that she won't be able to walk."

Miss Polly gasped. "Not walk? Do you mean that her legs are broken?" she asked.

He shook his head slowly. "I worry that it is much more serious than that." He packed up his bag and took his coat from the hook. "I'll come back in an hour or so to check on her. Try not to worry too much. She's a strong little girl."

Pollyanna slept through the next day. Miss Polly stayed by her side the entire time. Nancy even brought in a cot so Miss Polly could sleep in the room with her.

When Pollyanna finally woke up, she saw her aunt in a chair pulled close to the bed.

"Oh, Aunt Polly," she said. "I'm so sorry! I should never have run into the street. It was a silly, silly thing to do."

Miss Polly stroked the girl's hair. "You're right," she said gently. "It was a very silly thing to do. But you're safe now and finally awake. We've all been so worried about you."

"Have you?" Pollyanna asked. "I feel bad that I've made everyone worry. I want so much to get out of this bed and hug you, but I can't move. I must be so tired. Maybe I need to sleep some more. My legs feel too tired to move."

Pollyanna noticed that her aunt was crying.

"Is there something else wrong?"

Miss Polly could not speak.

"Is it my legs, Aunt Polly? Are they broken?" Pollyanna touched her aunt's cheek. "You shouldn't cry so much about broken legs, Aunt

Polly. They aren't really serious. Look at Mr. Pendleton. He had a broken leg and has improved greatly. It's nothing like Mrs. Snow. She will always be in bed because her legs don't work at all."

Just then Dr. Warren arrived for a checkup and Miss Polly was spared from saying anything else.

When the doctor left Pollyanna's room, Miss Polly pulled him aside for a quiet talk.

"I don't want Pollyanna to know how serious this is," she said. "Not until we have all the answers. She's a little girl and this is very hard for her."

"I understand," Dr. Warren said. "I've made arrangements for a special doctor to visit. He'll arrive tomorrow afternoon. He'll be able to tell if Pollyanna will ever walk again."

Miss Polly turned away quickly. All of this was too much to bear. Pollyanna was such a sweet and extraordinary child. It was hard to think of her in pain.

Miss Polly went back into Pollyanna's room. She told her niece that a special doctor would visit her tomorrow.

"Dr. Chilton?" Pollyanna said. Even though she was very tired, she was excited to see Dr. Chilton.

"No, dear," Miss Polly said. "Dr. Chilton will not be coming. It's another doctor. He's from the city. Dr. Warren said that he would be able to fix your legs."

"But Dr. Chilton could fix my legs," Pollyanna pleaded. "He fixed Mr. Pendleton's broken leg. He'll be able to fix my broken legs just as easily."

"I'm sorry," Miss Polly said. Her eyes filled with tears again. "I will give you anything you need. I will do everything possible to make you comfortable. But I am sorry, I cannot bring you Dr. Chilton. Please don't ask me again."

Pollyanna nodded her head. Although she

did not understand, she knew that her aunt was very stubborn.

❧

People started to visit the next morning. Millie Snow was the first to come. She brought a bunch of flowers wrapped with a red ribbon.

"I'm sorry to bother you, Miss Harrington," she said. "Mother and I heard that Miss Pollyanna was in an accident. We were very worried. Is she all right?"

"We're still waiting to hear from the doctor," Miss Polly said. "Would you like to come in?"

"Oh, no," Millie said. "I'm sure you're very busy. We just wanted you to know how much Pollyanna means to us. You wouldn't believe the change in Mother. No more dark rooms and old bedclothes for her! Her room is filled with sunlight now, and she wears ribbons in her hair. And it's all because of your niece."

Miss Polly did not know how to respond. She did not realize how much time Pollyanna had spent with Mrs. Snow. Or that Mrs. Snow was feeling happier. She thanked Millie for the flowers.

"I'll tell Pollyanna that you stopped by," she said.

"Thank you, ma'am," Millie said. She bowed slightly before heading home.

The doorbell rang all day. As soon as the townsfolk heard about Pollyanna's accident, they headed to the Harrington Estate. There were many people who Miss Polly had never met. Shopkeepers, schoolteachers, people from the church and the Ladies' Aid arrived with flowers and kind words. Every one of them told Miss Polly that Pollyanna had helped them in some way. They all said their lives were better and brighter because of the little girl.

Miss Polly smiled. "I know," she replied to

each of them. "She has made my world a better and brighter place, too."

At that moment, Miss Polly realized that Pollyanna had changed her life. She complained about her constant talking and slamming of doors, but she had grown to love the little girl. She loved her more than she thought possible. She did not want to think of a house without Pollyanna's good cheer. Miss Polly had to admit that she would even miss the slamming of doors.

Pollyanna noticed the change in her aunt. Aunt Polly called her *dear* now. She sat with her all evening. She listened to Pollyanna's stories without rolling her eyes.

This is a good reason to be glad, Pollyanna thought. *It is certainly unpleasant to be stuck in this bed with broken legs, but Aunt Polly finally seems to be happy with me now. That makes me very glad, indeed.*

CHAPTER 15

Dr. Chilton

༄

The special doctor arrived the next day. He examined Pollyanna carefully, asking her many questions. When he was finished, he asked Miss Polly and Dr. Warren to speak with him in the hall. Miss Polly closed the bedroom door as she left.

Unfortunately, the door was left slightly open. This meant that Pollyanna could hear everything that was said in the hall.

The little girl listened in horror as the special doctor said she would never walk again. She heard her aunt start to cry. She heard Dr. Warren talk about medicine and nurses. Pollyanna started to scream. She did not stop screaming until her aunt was back at her side.

It was a very sad household. Everyone—even Old Tom and Timothy—spoke quietly. Everyone had tears in their eyes. It did not take long for the news to spread all over town. Soon everyone in Beldingsville was worried about poor Pollyanna. They all tried to play the glad game, but it was hard to do without Pollyanna's help.

One afternoon the doorbell rang. It was Mr. Pendleton. Miss Polly was shocked to see him. However, she was very polite and asked him to come into the living room.

"Thank you very much," he said. "It's been a long time since we've spoken."

"It has," Miss Polly said. She asked him to take a seat.

"No, thank you. I'll only be a moment," Mr. Pendleton said.

He cleared his throat. "First of all," he said, "I think I should apologize for things I said many years ago. I was hurt and angry, but I had no right to say them."

"Thank you," Miss Polly said. She smiled at him. "I owe you an apology, too. I was wrong, but proud. I was angry with my sister for choosing the reverend. And I was angry with you for saying hurtful things about my sister. I wanted to apologize immediately afterwards, but . . ."

"We both suffered from too much pride," Mr. Pendleton said. "But now we have Pollyanna. I wish there was something I could do for her. I've heard that she will never walk again."

Miss Polly hung her head. "Yes, it's true."

"I'm very sorry to hear that," he said softly. "I have news that I hope will make her happy. Please tell her that I've brought Jimmy Bean into my home. I know she was worried about him. And I know she was very worried about me.

Please let her know that Jimmy and I will now take care of each other."

"I'll let her know right away," Miss Polly said.

Mr. Pendleton walked to the front door. He tipped his hat to Miss Polly on his way out. "I only wish I had some jelly to give Miss Pollyanna. She was always so generous with the jelly."

Miss Polly laughed.

"Oh, I've almost forgotten," Mr. Pendleton said. "I brought something for Pollyanna." He reached into his pocket and pulled out a small package.

Miss Polly unwrapped it. "What is this?" she asked.

Mr. Pendleton laughed. "It's a prism. Pollyanna knows all about prisms. I hope she will enjoy this one." He smiled and turned away.

Miss Polly waved to Mr. Pendleton as he walked down the driveway. She walked upstairs and found Pollyanna knitting. The girl had knit several scarves and three hats since she began her time in bed. She planned to give them all to the children in the Orphans' Home.

When Miss Polly gave her Mr. Pendleton's gift, Pollyanna squealed with delight. "Oh, Aunt Polly!" she said. "Isn't it beautiful? Could you please hang it in my window? It will be so wonderful in the morning when the sun comes in."

Miss Polly told her niece that she would send Nancy up later to hang it. Then she told Pollyanna Mr. Pendleton's news. The girl gave another little squeal.

"Oh, Aunt Polly," she said brightly. "That is the finest news I've heard in such a long time!"

"I'm glad to see you smile," Miss Polly said.

"Are you truly glad, Aunt Polly," she asked. "I thought you didn't like the word *glad*."

"I'm learning to like many things these days," her aunt said and smiled.

"Then I think it's time you finally learned how to play the game."

"Whatever are you talking about, dear?" Miss Polly asked.

So at long last Pollyanna taught her aunt the Just Be Glad game. Pollyanna even mentioned her father. This time, however, Miss Polly did not stop her. They spent the rest of the afternoon playing the game and laughing.

⤴

The next morning, Miss Polly received yet another visitor. This time it was Jimmy Bean. She almost didn't recognize him. He was wearing clean, new clothes and his hair was combed and neat.

"I'm sorry to bother you," he said. "I had to run over and tell you important news."

"Is there anything wrong?" Miss Polly asked. She worried that something had happened to Mr. Pendleton.

"I know that it's wrong to listen in on people's conversations, but I couldn't help it. I was sitting on the front porch and the window was open so I could hear everything. Dr. Chilton was very upset, so he came to talk to Mr. Pendleton. The doctor said that he knows another doctor who could help Pollyanna. He said this doctor is the best there is and he wants to bring him here. But Dr. Chilton was worried that you wouldn't agree because you don't like talking to him. That's why the doctor came to talk to Mr. Pendleton. He thought Mr. Pendleton could talk you into it."

"Where is Dr. Chilton now?" Miss Polly asked. Her voice sounded very excited.

"He's still at Mr. Pendleton's. They were still talking about it when I ran over here. I got excited and didn't want to waste time."

"You're a very smart boy, Jimmy Bean," she said. "Run back to Mr. Pendleton's right away. Run as fast as you can. Bring Dr. Chilton back here." Miss Polly opened the front door. "Hurry now!"

Jimmy Bean raced down the driveway.

Although it felt like hours to Miss Polly, Dr. Chilton was in her house in a very short time. She took him straight up to Pollyanna's room.

The little girl was so happy to see the doctor.

She started to ask him all sorts of questions and to tell him all about her accident.

"I know all about it," he said gently. "I'd like to have a look at your legs, if you don't mind."

"No, I don't mind," she said softly.

When he was done examining Pollyanna, Dr. Chilton asked Miss Polly if he could talk to her for a moment. Miss Polly nodded, although she could not look at him. She kissed her niece on the forehead before leaving the room.

"I'll be back shortly," she said.

But she did not return for several hours. It was already nighttime by the time her aunt came back in the room. Pollyanna was already asleep.

Miss Polly knelt beside her bed. She touched Pollyanna on the arm, waking her gently.

"Dear, dear," she said. "Wake up. I have some very special news for you. Dr. Chilton has made arrangements to send you to a special hospital. You'll visit a doctor who will be able to help you. You will walk again, I promise."

Pollyanna was about to talk when her aunt stopped her.

"Wait, my dear," she said. "I have more news. I think it will make you very happy. Dr. Chilton is going to come and live with us. He will be your uncle! Oh, Pollyanna, I can't thank you enough.

There was a time when he and I were going to be married. But we fought—I don't even remember why—and stopped talking. For so many years I tried to forget. I refused all contact with him—until you arrived. Oh, my darling Pollyanna, you brought us together! I have never been so glad!"

Pollyanna wrapped her arms around her aunt's neck and hugged tightly. "Oh, Aunt Polly," she sighed. "I don't think I have ever been so glad, either."

CHAPTER 16

The Letter

∽

Dearest Aunt Polly,

You will not believe what happened yesterday. I walked five steps! Five steps. Can you believe it? Everyone here was very proud of me. They all clapped and cheered. Even Old Emily, who cleans the floors, told me that I did a good job.

The doctor said I would be able to come home in a couple of months. I'm trying very hard to keep up with my studies so that I can stay with my class next year. One of the nurses is helping me with spelling. She said she would check this letter before I send it.

It was so wonderful to see you last month. And it was extra nice that you and Dr. Chilton—I mean Uncle Tom—got married right here in the hospital. I don't think anyone has been married among these hospital beds before. Everyone is still talking about it.

I miss you terribly. Please say hello to everyone—especially Nancy, Mr. Pendleton, and Jimmy.

I love you!
Pollyanna

What Do *You* Think?
Questions for Discussion

❧

Have you ever been around a toddler who keeps asking the question "Why?" Does your teacher call on you in class with questions from your homework? Do your parents ask you questions about your day at the dinner table? We are always surrounded by questions that need a specific response. But is it possible to have a question with no right answer?

The following questions are about the book you just read. But this is not a quiz! They are designed to help you look at the people, places, and events in the story from different angles. These questions do not have specific answers. Instead, they might make you think of the story in a completely new way.

Think carefully about each question and enjoy discovering more about this classic story.

1. Aunt Polly is willing to take Pollyanna in, but she isn't very warm toward her. Why do you think this is? Have you ever known anyone who acts like Aunt Polly?

2. How does Pollyanna react when she learns that Nancy is not her aunt? Why do you suppose Nancy is hesitant to tell her the truth? Have you ever been unsure how to tell someone something? Did you finally tell them?

3. Why do you suppose Aunt Polly doesn't want to hear about Pollyanna's father? How does Pollyanna react to this? Have you ever been told not to talk about something?

4. Why is Pollyanna glad to have no mirror in her room? Which of your features do you least like to look at in the mirror? What is your favorite part of your appearance?

5. Why do you suppose Pollyanna is so eager to teach everyone the Just Be Glad game? Do you think it's always possible to find something to be glad about? What makes you glad?

6. Pollyanna explains to Aunt Polly that she needs time in her day for "living." Do you agree with her? How do you spend your free time?

7. Dr. Chilton tells Pollyanna that she has made quite a difference in many people's lives. Do you agree? Whose life do you think you have affected the most?

8. Why do you think Aunt Polly gets upset when Pollyanna tells Mr. Pendleton that Aunt Polly didn't send the jelly? Have you ever accidentally told someone something they shouldn't know?

9. Mr. Pendleton says, "You know, Miss Pollyanna, I think the greatest, most wonderful prism of them all is you." What do you suppose he means by this? Have you ever met anyone like Pollyanna?

10. Pollyanna has no secrets of her own, so it never occurs to her to keep other people's secrets. Do you think this is good or bad? Have you ever been asked to keep a secret?

Afterword

by Arthur Pober, Ed.D.

⁓

First impressions are important.

Whether we are meeting new people, going to new places, or picking up a book unknown to us, first impressions count for a lot. They can lead to warm, lasting memories or can make us shy away from any future encounters.

Can you recall your own first impressions and earliest memories of reading the classics?

Do you remember wading through pages and pages of text to prepare for an exam? Or were you the child who hid under the blanket to read with a flashlight, joining forces with Robin Hood to save Maid Marian? Do you remember only how long it took you to read a lengthy novel such as *Little Women*? Or did you become best friends with the March sisters?

Even for a gifted young reader, getting through long chapters with dense language can easily become overwhelming and can obscure the richness of the story and its characters. Reading an abridged, newly crafted version of a classic novel can be the gentle introduction a child needs to explore the characters and storyline without the frustration of difficult vocabulary and complex themes.

Reading an abridged version of a classic novel gives the young reader a sense of independence and the satisfaction of finishing a "grown-up" book. And when a child is engaged with and inspired by a classic story, the tone is set for further exploration of the story's themes, characters, history, and details. As a child's reading skills advance, the desire to tackle the original, unabridged version of the story will naturally emerge.

If made accessible to young readers, these stories can become invaluable tools for understanding themselves in the context of their families and social environments. This is why the Classic Starts series includes questions that stimulate discussion regarding the impact and social relevance of the characters and stories today. These questions can foster lively conversations between children and their parents or teachers. When we look at the issues, values, and standards of past times in terms of how we live now, we can appreciate literature's classic tales in a very personal and engaging way.

Share your love of reading the classics with a young child, and introduce an imaginary world real enough to last a lifetime.

Dr. Arthur Pober, Ed.D.

Dr. Arthur Pober has spent more than twenty years in the fields of early childhood and gifted education. He is the former principal of one of the world's oldest laboratory schools for gifted youngsters, Hunter College Elementary School, and former Director of Magnet Schools for the Gifted and Talented for more than 25,000 youngsters in New York City.

Dr. Pober is a recognized authority in the areas of media and child protection and is currently the U.S. representative to the European Institute for the Media and European Advertising Standards Alliance.

Explore these wonderful stories in our
Classic Starts™ library.

Oliver Twist

Pollyanna

The Prince and the Pauper

Rebecca of Sunnybrook Farm

The Red Badge of Courage

Robinson Crusoe

The Secret Garden

The Story of King Arthur and His Knights

The Strange Case of Dr. Jekyll and Mr. Hyde

The Swiss Family Robinson

The Three Musketeers

Treasure Island

The War of the Worlds

White Fang

The Wind in the Willows